Treasure Island

Acknowledgments
Artists Penko Gelev
Sotir Gelev

This edition first published in 2014 by Book House

Distributed by Black Rabbit Books
P.O. Box 3263
Mankato
Minnesota MN 56002

Cataloging-in-Publication Data is available from the Library of Congress

HB ISBN: 978-1-908973-91-7
PB ISBN: 978-1-905638-01-7

Photo credits:
page 45 © The Salariya Book Company Ltd, 2006
page 46 TopFoto.co.uk KPA
page 47 TopFoto.co.uk FP

Every effort has been made to trace copyright holders. The Salariya Book Company apologizes
for any omissions and would be pleased, in such cases, to add an acknowledgment in future editions.

Treasure Island

Robert Louis Stevenson

Illustrated by
Penko Gelev

BOOK HOUSE
a SALARIYA imprint

Retold by
Fiona Macdonald

Series created and designed by
David Salariya

If schooners, islands, and maroons,
And buccaneers, and buried gold,
And all the old romance, retold
Exactly in the ancient way,
Can please, as me they pleased of old,
The wiser youngsters of today:
So be it, and fall on!

Robert Louis Stevenson, Treasure Island

CHARACTERS

Jim Hawkins

Long John Silver,
an old sea cook

Doctor Livesey

Captain Smollett,
captain of the *Hispaniola*

Billy Bones,
an old sea captain

Ben Gunn,
a marooned man

Squire Trelawney,
a wealthy gentleman

Blind Pew,
pirate

Tom Redruth,
gamekeeper

Israel Hands,
coxswain

Jim's
mother

Tom Morgan,
crewman

Job Anderson,
crewman

Abraham Gray,
crewman

Mr. Arrow,
first mate

Black Dog,
pirate

Dick Johnson,
crewman

George Merry,
crewman

John
Hunter,

O'Brien,
crewman

STRANGER AT THE INN

All is quiet at the Admiral Benbow Inn – until a tall, weather-beaten stranger knocks at the door. It is Billy Bones, an old sea captain.

Billy Bones calls for rum and asks lots of questions. When he hears that the Inn has few visitors, he decides to stay for a while.

Jim, the landlord's son, has never seen anyone like Billy Bones. He's very curious about him.

All day, every day, Billy Bones stares silently out to sea. What's he looking for? Who's he waiting for? And why is he so nervous?

Billy Bones asks Jim to warn him when strangers arrive at the inn – especially if they are sailors.

Thinking about mysterious strangers gives Jim nightmares. He dreams of monsters and murderers.

Every night, Billy Bones tells tales of his adventures at sea. He's often drunk, and very rowdy.

Jim's father falls ill, so Doctor Livesey visits the inn. He tells Billy Bones to behave better. Billy Bones is furious, and threatens him.

1. weather-eye: To keep a close watch.

THE ADMIRAL BENBOW

Billy Bones patrols the cliffs.

This fog is dangerous. I can't see enemies approaching.

Jim is alone when a stranger enters the inn. It is Black Dog, an out-of-work sailor. He calls for rum – and asks about Billy Bones.

We'll give Bill a little surprise . . .

Jim is suspicious. He tries to warn Billy Bones. But Black Dog stops him.

Well, then, speak up; what is it?

When Billy Bones returns to the inn, he finds Black Dog waiting for him. He goes pale with shock but recovers quickly.

No, no, no, no.

Black Dog tells Billy to sit down. They call for rum, and send Jim away so he can't listen to their conversation. All of a sudden, a fierce quarrel breaks out.

If it comes to swinging, swing all, say I.[1]

They fight.

Are you hurt?

We'll be back to get you, Billy Bones!

Black Dog runs away, with blood pouring from his wounded shoulder. Billy Bones looks shaken.

I must get away from here.

He asks Jim for more rum. Jim hurries to fetch the drink. But while he's away, Billy Bones collapses. The noise has alarmed Jim's mother, who comes running in to help.

1. swinging: Being hanged.

Jim's mother calls Doctor Livesey. He tells Billy Bones he's had a stroke and needs to rest quietly.[1]

While Billy Bones recovers, he tells Jim about his life at sea. He says Black Dog and his old shipmates want to steal his treasure.

Suddenly, sadness strikes Jim's family. His father falls ill and dies. Now Jim is so busy he doesn't have time to worry about Billy.

While Jim and his mother mourn, Billy Bones helps himself to rum. It makes him even more fearful. He sits brooding, with sword in hand.

Then, one day, a mysterious blind beggar arrives at the inn. He seems weak and helpless, but really he's tough and cruel. Billy seems helpless to refuse his orders.

We'll do them yet.

Blind Pew presses a small square of paper into Billy Bones's hand. The effect is alarming.

Billy leaps to his feet and cries out his defiance to Jim. But even as he does so, he clutches his hand to his throat and falls to the floor.

Jim tries to help him, but it's too late – Billy Bones is dead! He's been killed by thundering apoplexy.[2] Even though Jim didn't like him, he had begun to feel sorry for Billy.

---

1. stroke: When a blood vessel inside the brain is damaged, causing the person to lose consciousness.
2. apoplexy: Another term for having a stroke. It also means a fit of extreme anger.

BILLY BONES'S SEA CHEST

Jim and his mother rush out of the inn, leaving Billy Bones dead on the floor. Where can they go? What can they do?

They hurry to the nearest village, and ask for help to arrest Blind Pew. But no one is brave enough!

Fearfully, Jim and his mother creep back to the inn. There's no sign of Blind Pew, but Billy Bones's body is still there.

It's the Black Spot! It warned Billy that he had until ten o'clock that night before the pirates came for the treasure.

Jim also finds a key, hung around Billy's neck. His mother tries it in the lock of the old sea chest Billy brought to the inn.

The chest contains clothes, a compass, guns – and very smelly tobacco. Hidden right at the bottom are a small, heavy bag and a mysterious packet.

Jim takes the packet. His mother opens the bag. It's full of real gold coins – more than enough to pay Billy's debts!

Suddenly, Jim hears a sinister, scary sound – a stick tap-tap-tapping at the inn's front door. Blind Pew is back . . . and he's not alone.

---

1. The doctor is also the local judge, so he would be able to help them. There was no police force at this time.
2. farthing: An old coin used in England in the 18th century.

"Take the money and run."

Jim and his mother have to run for their lives. Jim's mother soon gets tired and collapses. Jim hides her under a bridge.

"Aloft and get the chest."

Meanwhile, back at the inn, Blind Pew and his gang are smashing their way through the door. They are armed with deadly weapons.

"Is it there?"

"They've been before us!"

"Someone's turned the chest out."

They rush to Billy's room, to get his sea chest. They find it open – and empty!

"Scatter and find 'em! Rout the house out![1]"

"Thump!"

"Bang!"

"Crash!"

"Crack!"

The furious gang destroys the inn.

Suddenly they hear a blast from their lookout, warning them that the coast guard patrol are closing in on them.

"You won't leave old Pew, mates – not old Pew!"

"Run for your lives!"

"Back to our boat!"

"Aaaaaaaarghhh!!!"

The gang hear the coast guards approaching and escape. But they leave Blind Pew behind. Without them, he is helpless and stumbles into the path of a coast guard's horse.

"They'll be hunting for this packet."

"Let's ask the doctor what to do."

With Pew dead and the rest of the gang escaped, peace returns. But Jim is still worried. He warns the guards that the gang may come back.

1. "Rout the house": Search the house.

BURIED TREASURE

Jim and the guards arrive at the doctor's house but discover he is not at home. They ride on to the Hall, and find the doctor and the squire talking by the fireside.[1]

The coast guard tells the squire about Blind Pew and his gang. Then he goes home, leaving Jim behind at the Hall.

Jim shows the squire the mysterious packet he found in Billy Bones's sea chest.

The squire and the doctor examine the packet. They cut the strings that fasten it and open it very carefully. Inside, they find a book . . .

. . . and a map of a tropical island! The map is marked with compass directions and three red crosses.[2] The squire peers at these closely, then shouts out in excitement.

The squire soon realizes they've found the infamous Captain Flint's treasure map.

Captain Flint was the cruelest, cleverest, richest pirate who ever sailed the seas, and his treasure must be worth a fortune!

1. squire: The title given to the main landowner in an area. It's no longer used.
2. For a closer look at the map, see p. 44.
3. buccaneer: Another name for a pirate.

In three weeks time we'll have the best ship in England. . . . Hawkins shall be cabin boy.

This is Redruth, the squire's gamekeeper. He'll look after you.

The squire gets very excited and makes plans for an expedition. He'll buy a ship, hire a crew, and dig up Captain Flint's treasure!

The next day, the squire leaves for Bristol, the nearest big port. The doctor goes to care for his patients, while Jim stays behind at the Hall.

He's got a ship!

Jim is happy at the Hall. He feels safe from Blind Pew's gang. He spends his time studying Captain Flint's treasure map and dreaming of adventure.

One day, Jim gets a letter from the squire. It contains thrilling news – the Squire has bought a ship: the *Hispaniola*.

Farewell, my son! Take care!

Don't cry, Mother.

In the letter, the squire also says that the doctor is in London and will meet them in Bristol. He tells Jim to hurry and join them.

Jim is very excited, but his mother can't help worrying if she will ever see him again. So Jim sets out for Bristol, with trusty Redruth beside him as protection.

What will he find there? Who will he meet? And will he enjoy his adventure? As he says good-bye to his home, Jim spares a thought for poor Billy Bones.

LONG JOHN SILVER

Jim and Redruth arrive in Bristol and make their way to the harbor. They have never seen such fine ships – or seen so many strange-looking people.

They find the squire and the doctor waiting for them. The squire is in high spirits. He announces that he's hired a crew and the adventure will begin in the morning.

Long John welcomes Jim to his neat, clean inn. He seems kind and friendly. Jim soon forgets his worries – this can't be the man Billy feared!

The next day, Jim is sent to fetch Long John Silver, the ship's new cook. The squire tells him Silver only has one leg, and as Jim walks along the docks he worries this is the man Billy Bones was so afraid of.

But who's this, lurking in a dark corner? It's Black Dog, the old shipmate who threatened Billy Bones! When he sees Jim, he heads for the door and is soon outside and running.

Black Dog hadn't paid his bill, so Long John Silver sends two barmen to chase him. He seems very surprised to learn a pirate has been visiting his inn.

The barmen return, empty-handed. They've bad news to report – Black Dog got away! Silver tells Jim how ashamed he is he couldn't catch Black Dog himself.

Silver says he'll go with Jim to see the squire. As they walk along, he talks about the ships they see in the harbor.

Silver tells the squire how Black Dog ran away from his inn. He is worried that the squire will think he's friendly with pirates.

Later, the squire and the doctor discuss Long John Silver. They both like him and are looking forward to setting sail.

1. keelhaul: Being dragged through the water and along the underside (keel) of a ship.

15

THE ADVENTURE BEGINS

The ship is ready!

This is so exciting!

Jim goes on board with the squire and the doctor. They are welcomed by Mr. Arrow, the first mate.[1] A weather-beaten old sailor, he's second-in-command and seems honest.

I don't like this cruise, I don't like the men, and I don't like my officer.

Next, they meet Captain Smollett. He's brisk, stern, and clever. In the past, he's led many successful voyages. But right now he's angry!

I've heard you have a map of an island . . .

I never told that to a soul!

The squire has not yet told the captain of his plans to find Flint's treasure. But the crew seem to know all about it.

Let me take certain precautions or let me resign.

You fear a mutiny?[2]

If the crewmen know too much, they'll take the treasure for themselves!

The captain is horrified when he hears the squire's plans. He warns that treasure hunting is very risky. They might all be killed!

The captain agrees to stay. But he insists that they hide the map of the island and keep all their plans secret from the crew, if they can.

1. first mate: The officer on a ship who is second-in-command to the captain.
2. mutiny: When the crew of a ship rebel and take control from the captain.

Jim watches as the crewmen hoist the sails and load the ship with food and water. They'll sail on the next tide.

Soon, a friendly face peers over the ship's side. It's Long John Silver! As he scrambles on board, the crew hurry to greet him.

Long John salutes Captain Smollett, who orders him belowdecks to start cooking right away.

At last the stores are all aboard, and it's time to leave port. The crewmen turn the heavy capstan that hauls up the anchor.[1]

To help them work, Long John Silver sings. Jim remembers that he's heard the song before – from the old pirate, Billy Bones!

---

1. capstan: The wheel that the anchor cable is wound around to either lower or raise the anchor.

OUTWARD VOYAGE

Their long journey starts well, with fine weather and calm seas. The ship sails south and west, out into the Atlantic Ocean.

Jim enjoys life on board. The crew are friendly, the captain is an excellent commander, and even Silver's cooking tastes good!

Most of the crew work hard, but Mr. Arrow is drunk for most of the time. One night he disappears, and it's assumed that he's fallen overboard.

Mr. Arrow is replaced by two senior crewmen: Job Anderson and Israel Hands. They take over the important task of steering the ship.

Hands is an old friend of Silver's. They've often sailed together. He says Silver is fierce and strong – and as brave as a lion. The entire crew seems to like and respect him, including Jim.

Silver is always pleased to see Jim and loves to talk about great sailors and epic voyages. He describes rich treasure ships, laden with silks, spices, jewels, and golden coins.

1. yarn: A seafaring term for talking.

Pieces of eight!
Pieces of eight![1]

Something's not right.
I fear trouble.

I call her 'Captain Flint,'
after the famous buccaneer.
He was wicked!

Silver says his parrot is 200 years old and has spent her life at sea. Like him, she's seen battles, shipwrecks, and tons of treasure!

Jim is happy – though he wonders why the name 'Captain Flint' makes him feel uneasy. But not everyone on board is happy.

Spoil forecastle hands,
make devils.[2]

Squire says we can
help ourselves!

The squire and the captain still don't like each other. They frequently quarrel, and when the squire gives the crew extra rations of cake and rum, the captain is angry.

But the squire ignores the captain's advice, and offers the crew free apples. These are stored on deck in a huge wooden barrel.

I can reach them
if I climb inside.

I can hear voices.
There's someone
coming!

Yawn.

The voyage is going well, and one evening when Jim has finished his work, he goes to fetch an apple. Finding there are not many left, he climbs in to reach the bottom.

There's lots of room inside, and it's a good place to shelter from wind and sea spray. Jim eats his apple, then becomes sleepy from the rocking of the waves. He dozes off.

Suddenly, he awakes . . .

---

1. Pieces of eight: The name of an old Spanish silver coin.
2. Spoil: The captain warns that being too kind to the crew will keep them from having respect for him.

MUTINY!

Flint was cap'n; I was quartermaster, along of my timber leg.[1]

I'll finish with them at the island as soon as the blunt's on board.[2]

The voices Jim hears belong to Silver, Israel Hands, and Dick Johnson. To his horror he learns they were part of Flint's pirate crew!

They plan to mutiny, take over the ship and dispose of the squire, captain, and doctor. After that, they plan to keep Flint's treasure for themselves.

They'll kill us all!

It'll be like the good old days!

Wait is what I say, but when the time comes, let her rip!

Jim is still hiding inside the barrel, and what he hears fills him with terror. They're so cold-hearted! What will he do?

Hands wants to strike quickly; he's angry at having to follow the captain's orders. Dick wonders if they should maroon the squire and his friends or just kill them.[3]

Silver convinces Hands that it's much better to let Captain Smollett get them to the island, and to use the extra men to carry the treasure on board before killing them.

Let's drink to luck . . . and old Flint.

He warns the mutineers to keep their plans secret until it's time to take action.

Excited by their hopes of finding Captain Flint's treasure, the mutineers start drinking. They tell bloodthirsty stories of past pirate raids.

1. quartermaster: A low-ranking officer responsible for steering a ship.
2. blunt: Treasure.
3. maroon: Abandoning someone on an island.

Not another man of them'll jine.[1]

Dick leaves, and Jim hears Hands whispering to Silver. He only manages to hear a few words of what is said, but what he does hear gives him hope.

There are still **some** faithful men on board.

There are some men on board that the pirates have not managed to turn against the captain. But whom can Jim trust?

Suddenly . . .

LAND HO!

"... It were a main place for pirates once."

Skeleton Island they calls it. . . .

It's the island! Everyone rushes up to the main deck to have a good look.

They want to kill you, too!

We're in terrible danger!

Doctor, I have terrible news.

We must go on, because we can't turn back.

While everyone else is busy looking at the island, Jim has a private word with the doctor.

Jim tells the doctor about the planned mutiny – and that most of the crew seem to be pirates!

The doctor takes Jim straight to the captain's cabin. Jim tells the captain, doctor, and squire all he has heard.

1. jine: Join.

TREASURE ISLAND

The ship sails on, closer to the island. Captain Smollett asks the crew what they know about Flint and his treasure. He wants to know who the pirates are, and whom he can trust.

The captain shows the crew a copy he has made of Billy Bones's map. The mutineers all pretend not to have seen it before. Silver must be disappointed it isn't Billy Bones's map, but he hides it well.

At dawn the next day, the island is clearly visible. To Jim it seems strange and desolate.[1]

The ship sails closer to the shore, then carefully drops anchor in the dangerous waters.

The mutineers among the crew are restless and surly. Silver tries to keep them in order, and is even more cheerful and helpful to the captain.

The captain tells the crew that they can go ashore. They are delighted. Meanwhile, he tells Hunter, Joyce, and Redruth of the plot against them.

Thirteen of the crew climb into the boats and head for the island . . . but they leave six men behind on the *Hispaniola*.

The six mutineers are given orders to stay alert but not to act against the captain without Silver's order.

1. desolate: Deserted and lifeless.

Like the crew, Jim wants to explore the island. He stows away on one of the boats, hoping that no one will see him.[1]

Jim, is that you?

But Silver quickly spots him, and is angry. Jim is scared and starts to regret his foolishness.

As soon as the boats reach the shore, Jim leaps out and runs to hide in the jungle. Silver calls out to him, but Jim keeps running.

Jim runs on and on . . .

Sounds like a spinning top.

He sees giant plants and strange, wild animals. In a forest clearing, he comes face to face with a deadly rattlesnake.

If I die like a dog, I'll die in my dooty.[2]

Suddenly Jim hears voices. It's Silver and one of the crewmen who refuses to mutiny. Silver tries to convince the man, but then in the distance they hear a terrible scream.

The terrified crewman starts to run. Silver takes out his knife and throws a heavy branch that knocks the crewman to the ground, where he lies dazed.

Aghast, Jim watches as Silver stabs him, the effort leaving him breathless. Soon the crewman is dead.

Jim faints from the shock of witnessing this brutal murder. When he wakes, his mind fills with fears that Silver will kill him, too.

1. stows away: Hides on a ship.
2. dooty: Duty – the crewman will not betray Captain Smollett.

BEN GUNN

Jim gets up and starts running. He's filled with terror and desperate to get away from Long John Silver.

A sudden sound makes Jim stop, terrified. He looks ahead and sees a shadowy shape leaping through the trees.

Luckily Jim remembers his gun! The captain gave it to him when he heard of the crew's plans to mutiny. Now Jim bravely steps forward.

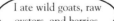

Slowly the shadowy shape comes closer. Could it be a cannibal? No, it's a wild and ragged-looking man who begs Jim for mercy.

Kneeling, the man tells Jim that he's a British sailor, and his name is Ben Gunn.

Ben Gunn tells Jim that he's the first person he's spoken to in three long years.

He was marooned. Since then, his life has been hard and lonely, but he has survived.

He's made clothes from goatskins and old sails, a rough shelter, and a little boat. Mysteriously, he also claims to have found a fortune!

"So much I'll tell you and no more."

Ben Gunn explains that he was an old shipmate of Long John Silver, Billy Bones, Blind Pew, and Captain Flint.

Flint and six of the crew went ashore to bury the treasure . . .

. . . but Flint returned alone.

"But there he was, and the six all dead."

Three years later, when Ben saw the island with a different crew of pirates, he suggested they look for Flint's treasure. When they found nothing, they marooned him.

"Not a man with one leg?"

Jim tells Ben that some of Flint's old crew are on the island, and Ben reveals that he too is scared of Long John Silver.

Jim asks Ben Gunn to come with him to meet the captain and squire. He knows they'll help Ben Gunn travel back to Britain, and they can all share the treasure.

"Ben Gunn has reasons of his own."

Ben Gunn is scared and runs away into the trees. But he tells Jim not to worry, and that he will find him again.

A SAFE SHELTER?

Nervously, Jim heads back to the shore. On the way, he spots a wooden cabin, surrounded by a stockade.

While Jim is talking to Ben Gunn, the captain, doctor and squire take one of the boats and escape to shore. Abraham Gray struggles free from the pirates to rejoin his captain.

The pirates on board try very hard to stop them. Israel Hands, who was Flint's gunner, readies the cannon to shoot.[1]

The squire is the best shot and tries to shoot Hands, but misses, hitting one of the other pirates instead.

The pirates shoot at the captain's jolly boat, hoping to sink it.[2] But the loyal crew members, Hunter, Joyce, Redruth, and Gray, row hard and steer so that the cannonballs land harmlessly in the sea.

As the boat reaches the island, the captain wades ashore and heads for the stockade. He knows how to find it from Billy Bones's map.

But the main gang of pirates is hiding nearby, ready to ambush and kill them. They attack!

After a short gunfight, the pirates run away, but Redruth, the squire's faithful gamekeeper, is badly wounded.

1. gunner: The person in charge of firing the cannons.
2. jolly boat: A medium-sized boat used to bring people ashore.

The captain leads the way to the cabin. Once there, they take stock of the provisions they've managed to save.

"That will show them!"

Captain Smollett takes the British flag from his pocket and climbs to the roof to run it up in defiance of the pirates.[1]

"The rations are very short."

Together, the captain and the doctor discuss food supplies. The consort could not be expected to reach them for several months.[2]

BOOM! BANG!

Their discussions are interrupted by cannon fire from the ship. They can't see the cabin but are aiming at the flag! At this moment . . .

"I am not sure whether he is sane."

. . . Jim leaps over the stockade to rejoin his friends. He describes his meeting with Ben Gunn and repeats all that he has learned.

The captain sets the loyal crewmen to work. The food supplies are so low, the captain is worried they'll be starved out.

"Captain says it's good for us to keep busy."

The men dig a grave for their fallen shipmate, Redruth, and gather plenty of firewood for cooking and warmth.

Sadly, they bury poor Tom Redruth – a good man killed in the struggle to get hold of Captain Flint's pirate treasure. Privately, each person wonders how many more will die.

1. run it up: Attaching a flag to a pole.
2. consort: The rescue ship which would be sent once it was noted the *Hispaniola* was late returning to Bristol.

SWORN ENEMIES

The captain, doctor, and squire meet to make plans. They decide to stay in the stockade and kill the pirates one by one.

But the very next morning, Long John Silver arrives at the stockade waving a flag of truce.[1] He says he wants peace and is now using the name "Captain" Silver!

These lads chose me cap'n after your desertion, sir.

We want that treasure, and we'll have it.

The captain refuses to let Silver enter the cabin, but listens quietly to the mutineers' peace terms: They want Billy Bones's map.

In return, they will let the captain and his men back on board the ship. They promise no harm will come to them.

No!

Refuse, and you've seen the last of me but musket balls.

They sit on the ground and Silver tries to persuade him, but the captain stays firm. When Silver issues threats, the captain orders the pirate out of the stockade.

Them that die'll be the lucky ones.

Silver asks for help to stand, but nobody comes forward. He's forced to crawl to the cabin where he can pull himself upright. He's furious and curses the captain and his men.

I've no manner of doubt that we can drub them, if you choose.[2]

It's war! The captain warns that the pirates will soon attack the stockade. He warns his men to prepare for the pirates.

1. truce: A temporary halt to fighting.
2. drub: Defeat.

The pirates surround the stockade. They are all armed with guns and deadly cutlasses.[1]

Inside, the captain and his men get ready to fight for their lives.

The battle begins! The pirates rush over the stockade and charge toward the captain's men.

Aaargggghhhhhh!

Fight 'em in the open!

The fighting is fast and furious. Jim bravely takes part. Hunter is knocked unconscious, Joyce is sadly killed, but they manage to kill five of the pirates.

Look! The captain's wounded!

Have they run?

At last the battle is over, and the pirates limp away to their camp on the shore. But the captain's men have suffered great losses and are still in danger. . . .

1. Cutlasses: Short swords with curved blades used by pirates.

JIM'S SEA ADVENTURE

Next morning.

I hope he can help us.

Hunter dies overnight without waking. The doctor tends the captain's wounds, then sets off into the woods to try and find Ben Gunn.

During the night, Jim has also thought of a plan. He takes guns and food, and while the others are occupied . . .

. . . he climbs over the stockade and hurries to the shore. He wants to find Ben Gunn's boat and escape from the island. He hides until nightfall.

That's the PIRATE flag!

Later that night.

Jim finds Ben Gunn's homemade boat, then sees the *Hispaniola* at anchor. It's flying the Jolly Roger![1]

It's very small, even for me.

With great difficulty, Jim carries Ben Gunn's little goatskin boat down to the water.

But it's VERY heavy!

I'm sinking!

Jim climbs aboard, then paddles toward the ship. The sea is rough, and Jim struggles to keep control. The coracle is safe, yet it has an alarming habit of twisting around and around in the water, which makes it hard to steer.[2]

Jim reaches the ship – and hacks away at the anchor rope until there are only a few strands left holding it.

30   1. Jolly Roger: The pirate flag. It was often a black background with a white skull and crossbones.
      2. coracle: A small round boat made of material stretched over a wooden frame.

From above, Jim can hear the sound of men drinking and quarrelling. It's Hands and another man, O'Brien, and both sound drunk.

At last, the rope breaks, and the ship floats free. The men on board have not noticed!

Quickly, Jim grabs the end of the rope and climbs up it like a monkey! He leaves Ben Gunn's boat behind, empty, on the water.

Jim reaches the edge of the ship's main deck. Cautiously, he peers over. The watchmen are too busy fighting to notice.

Without an anchor, the ship floats free. . . .

At last the mutineers on board realize what is happening! They rush to the ship's side and peer over. What they see fills them with fear.

Jim fears the men will see him. So he climbs back down into Ben Gunn's boat and falls asleep exhausted, only to dream of the Admiral Benbow Inn.

31

DEADLY PERIL

Oh no!

The next morning.

Jim sleeps for hours – and wakes to find himself surrounded by high waves. Ben Gunn's boat bobs and swirls uncontrollably.

Worse still, strange monsters are lurking close to the shore. To Jim they look like giant slugs, but he finds out later that they're harmless sea lions!

That's our ship! Adrift! It's coming this way!

Jim leaps for his life as the ship crashes into Ben Gunn's boat. He scrambles on board . . .

Brandy.

. . . where a terrible sight meets his eyes: two men, both covered in blood. One is dead, the other is still alive . . . just. He manages to utter only one word.

What a mess!

The living man is Israel Hands, one of the leading pirates. Feeling sorry for the dying man, Jim goes to fetch him some brandy.

I've come aboard to take possession of this ship.

Hands sits up and drinks, but he's still very weak. Jim seizes the chance to take control.

And there's an end to Captain Silver!

He hauls the pirates' Jolly Roger down from the mast. Jim and the wounded pirate strike a deal to help each other.

Jim tries to steer the ship to safety, and grumbling all the time, Israel Hands tells him what to do. They sail the *Hispaniola* along the coast of the island.

32

Jim dresses Hands's wounds, and the pirate starts to recover. When he thinks Jim's not looking, he grabs a short dirk.[2] Jim notices that Hands often watches him carefully.

Together, Jim and Hands steer the ship toward the shore. Hands issues orders for landing the ship, and Jim is kept busy . . .

. . . but something makes him turn, and he sees Hands advancing, dirk in hand. He's been pretending to be weaker than he is! As he attacks, Jim runs up the mizzen shrouds.[3]

Hands climbs after him, but his wounded leg makes progress slow and painful. This gives Jim time to load his guns. But Hands throws a knife that hits Jim in the shoulder.

Panicked, Jim fires his guns, and Hands cries out, losing his hold.

Hands falls into the sea dead. Jim feels sick and terrified but finds the strength to climb down from the rigging.

Luckily his wound is not serious, because Jim must now steer the ship alone, and try to reach dry land safely.

He loses control and the ship runs aground. Jim climbs off, and heads inland to try to find the captain, squire, and doctor . . . if they are still alive.

1. "Dead men don't bite": Dead men are no danger.
2. dirk: A dagger.
3. mizzen shrouds: The ropes attached to the mizzenmast.

ENEMY CAMP

Jim walks inland. What's that red glow he can see? Surely Ben Gunn isn't being so careless with his cookfire. . . .

Keeping low, Jim creeps up to the cabin in the center of the stockade. He's amazed that nobody appears to be keeping lookout.

He hears men snoring and tiptoes quietly inside, expecting to find the captain, doctor, and squire.

But suddenly Jim finds himself surrounded by pirates! They've taken over the stockade. The captain, doctor, and squire are now sheltering in Ben Gunn's cave.

Long John Silver demands to know what Jim's been doing since they last met.

He says that the captain, doctor, and squire are angry with Jim for running off without a word and leaving them. Jim's horrified that his friends have turned against him.

He confesses that he's been behind all the pirates' failures: The men left on board are dead, and the *Hispaniola*'s adrift!

When the pirates hear this, they become very angry. They want to kill Jim right away, but Silver persuades them to spare the boy.

34

The pirates are furious with Silver for protecting Jim from their revenge. They turn on him, sneering and cursing. They threaten him, but Silver is unafraid and dares them to attack him.

The pirates huddle together and hold a council of war. Every now and then they look over to where Silver and Jim are standing.

Silver tells Jim that both their lives are in danger, and the pirates are now both their enemies. He promises to save Jim, if in turn Jim saves him from hanging.

The pirates decide to give Silver the Black Spot which they cut from a Bible. Silver turns the paper over and sees the word "Deposed."

Like Billy Bones before him, Silver knows he is in trouble and must think quickly to survive.

But he's clever and brave, and argues with the pirates about why he should stay captain. Eventually he strikes a deal with them.

If they spare his life – and Jim's – Silver will give them Billy Bones's treasure map. The doctor handed it to him when he left the stockade. The pirates can't believe their luck, and they leap upon the map, cheering and praising Long John Silver.

1. Deposed: No longer wanted as captain.

THE SKELETON'S SECRET

Not Jim?

Daybreak next morning.

The boy'll tell you how I saved his life.

Next day, the doctor calls at the stockade. He's come to check on the wounded pirates and is amazed to find Jim there. After the doctor has treated the men, he says he wants to talk to Jim alone.

Silver tells him that he must step outside the stockade while he and Jim talk. He also tells the doctor how he saved Jim and seems to be trying to be friendly.

Whip over, and we'll run for it.

Don't you be in any great hurry after that treasure.

The doctor tells Jim he must try to escape. He wants him to jump over the fence and make a run for freedom. But Jim gave his word not to escape and has to refuse.

The doctor tells Jim that they've found Ben Gunn, and then gives him a mysterious warning. . . .

Then he walks away, to join the captain and the squire back in Ben Gunn's cave. He tells Silver to keep Jim close to him.

They row along the coast . . .

Now that they've got the map, the pirates are desperate to dig up Captain Flint's treasure.

They tie a rope around Jim, which Silver holds, leading him like a dancing bear.

. . . then march inland, using clues marked on Billy Bones's map to guide them.

They find the the first clue – a tall pine tree – but then there's a horrid surprise!

They see the skeleton of a man stretched out on the ground. He seems to be lying in an odd way, almost as if he was pointing to something . . .

He's dead and gone below.[1]

He died bad, did Flint!

The dead man must be one of the six men killed by Captain Flint. The pirates remember how cruel the captain was.

Aaargh! It's Flint!

What's that?

But then they're terrified to hear a thin, eerie voice singing. They believe it's the ghost of wicked Captain Flint come to haunt them!

Fifteen men on the dead man's chest …

(It's really Ben Gunn, hiding in the bushes!)

That fixes it! Let's go!

As they're fleeing, Silver calls them back.

Someone's been here before us!

Silver convinces them that it wasn't Flint they heard, and they all hurry on to the spot where Captain Flint buried his treasure. But when they arrive, they find an empty hole—the treasure's gone!

1. gone below: Gone to Hell.

HEADING HOME

The pirates are dumbstruck. They howl with rage and fury and quickly turn against Silver again. As they raise their weapons and advance, Jim thinks there is no hope.

But then there's a blaze of gunfire from the bushes behind them. Some pirates fall to the ground. Jim and Long John Silver survive!

It's the doctor, Abe Gray, and Ben Gunn who have been hiding in the bushes with their guns. The doctor is eager to prevent the pirates' escape.

The remaining pirates make a run for the shore, followed by Jim, Silver, and the doctor.

As they hurry along, Ben Gunn tells Silver how he discovered the treasure by accident one day.

He discovered the treasure years ago, dug it up, and carried it sack by sack, up to his cave.

Billy Bones's map was useless all the time! That's why the doctor gave it to Silver – and also why they abandoned the stockade!

Now Jim must help his friends find the *Hispaniola* so they can carry all of Flint's treasure back to England. They set off in the jolly boat to row along the coast.

As they look up to the cliffs by Ben's cave, they see the squire waiting to greet them. They cheer with happiness, including Long

They find the *Hispaniola* drifting close to the shore. It's slightly damaged, but still seaworthy.

Dead men hang about your neck like millstones.

Silver salutes the squire, which angers him, and he makes his dislike of the cunning old pirate very clear. But as Silver saved Jim, the squire has agreed not to prosecute him.

The squire says Silver must help load the ship with treasure. Jim wonders how much blood has been spilled for the gold.

Nearly every variety of money in the world must be here.

Don't go!

We're maroooooooned!

Jim helps by sorting the glittering gold coins into bulging, clinking sackfuls. There are gold coins from all over the world.

Soon it's time to go. They leave the remaining three pirates behind. The captain can't risk another mutiny, and if they returned to England, they'd be hanged anyway.

As for the wily pirate, Long John Silver, he is a friendly and helpful sea cook again. But, at their first port of call in South America, he escapes with a sackful of gold and is never seen again.

Jim, Ben Gunn, the captain, doctor, and squire arrive safely back in Bristol and divide up the remaining gold. But Jim can't forget all he's done or seen, and no power in Heaven or on Earth could make him go back to the island that still haunts his most terrifying nightmares.

The End

ROBERT LOUIS STEVENSON (1850 – 1894)

Robert Louis Stevenson was born in Edinburgh on November 13, 1850. He was the only son of Thomas Stevenson and wife Margaret Isabella Balfour. Both families were wealthy, well-educated, and deeply respectable. His mother suffered from tuberculosis, and it is unclear if she passed the disease on to Robert or if he suffered from another lung disorder. Either way, he was often too ill to attend school and thus lay in bed, reading or composing poems and stories of his own.

Robert Louis Stevenson, from an image held at Bishop Museum, Hawaii.

UNIVERSITY

At 17, he enrolled at Edinburgh University. His father wanted him to study engineering, but Robert wanted only to be a writer. As a compromise, he studied law but spent all his spare time writing. During vacations, he travelled to France to meet other young artists and writers. He was often ill but always lively, unconventional, and determined.

MARRIAGE

In 1875, Robert qualified as a lawyer but never worked in the profession. His first book, about a canoe expedition in France, was published in 1878, and he spent the rest of his life as a writer. In France, Robert also met the woman who would later become his wife: Fanny Van de Grift Osbourne, an American. They were a strange couple, but passionately in love. She was everything he was not: loud, healthy, and vibrant. Robert's family was not happy because Fanny was 11 years older than Robert and was already married. In 1880, after Fanny's divorce, Robert travelled to America to marry her. Robert's family was appalled, but the couple was happy together.

First Novel

In 1881, Robert and Fanny travelled to Scotland with Fanny's son, Lloyd Osbourne. They made peace with Robert's family and visited the Highlands with them. But the cold and rain worsened Robert's health, and they soon left in search of milder weather. They travelled to Switzerland, France, and the south of England, then back to America. All the time, Robert wrote – travel books, poems, and short stories. Then, in 1883, he published his first long novel. Its title was *Treasure Island*. During the next six years, Robert wrote four more novels. These included his most famous work, *The Strange Case of Dr. Jekyll and Mr. Hyde*. A brilliant fantasy thriller, it was an instant best-seller and made him famous throughout Britain and America.

Deteriorating Health

By 1887 Robert's health was getting worse, so he and Fanny returned to America with his mother (his father had died). Then with Fanny's children they set sail across the Pacific Ocean.

Samoa

After a long voyage they settled on the island of Samoa. They built a house and made friends with islanders, who called Robert "Tusitala" ("Teller of Tales"). Robert was fascinated by the islands and their rich heritage of songs and stories. He collected information for a huge history of the Pacific, campaigned to stop Europeans' ill-treatment of local people, and wrote poems and stories about the island. Robert also wrote novels set in faraway Scotland. The last of these, *Weir of Hermiston*, which he never finished, was probably his best piece of writing. Sadly, even the warm Pacific climate could not cure Robert's illness, and he died suddenly, on December 3, 1894 – just 44 years old. He was buried on the top of Mount Vaea, above his home in Samoa, and lines from his own poem, *Requiem*, were carved on his tomb:

"Under the wide and starry sky,
Dig the grave and let me lie.
Glad did I live and gladly die,
And I laid me down with a will."

A photograph of Robert Louis Stevenson's tomb on Mt. Vaea, Samoa.

BACKGROUND TO THE BOOK

THE STORY BEHIND *TREASURE ISLAND*

Robert Louis Stevenson spent the summer of 1881 with his family at a village in the Scottish Highands. While there, he began writing a story about pirates based on a game he played to amuse his stepson, Lloyd Osbourne. Lloyd and Stevenson pretended to be pirates and have exciting adventures. Together, they also drew a wonderful map of an imaginary "Treasure Island."

Later that year in Switzerland, Stevenson wrote his story down in seventeen short episodes. He gave them a title, *The Sea Cook*, and sold them to a publishing company for just £30. They were printed, week by week, in a children's magazine called *Young Folks*. The publishers hid his identity behind a false name: Captain Robert North. They thought that adults who knew his earlier travel writings might think less of him for writing children's books!

In 1883, all the episodes were collected together and re-published in book form.

Stevenson changed some of the text and chose a new title: *Treasure Island*. This was Stevenson's first full-length book, and he wrote it very quickly, completing a chapter every day. He intended it to be a simple, enjoyable story with (in his words) "no fine writing." He expected it to be read only by boys of about the same age as Lloyd. But good sales encouraged Stevenson to write more novels.

Adults also liked reading *Treasure Island*. It was action-packed, and featured an exotic, faraway setting. Its story line was fast-paced and full of unexpected surprises. The characters in it seemed real, a mixture of good and bad, brave and cowardly. Stevenson said he often based his characters on real people. For example, Long John Silver was inspired by a deceitful sailor who used to work for his father. He also drew on memories of adventure books he had read and enjoyed, such as *Robinson Crusoe* (1719). He also learned from histories of real-life pirates, such as the notorious Blackbeard (real name Edward Teach, who died in 1718), who was believed to have buried a fabulous hoard of treasure.

Buccaneer of the Caribbean *by Howard Pyle (1853–1911)*.

TREASURE ISLAND

PAST AND PRESENT VIEWS

*I*t is over 120 years since *Treasure Island* was first published. During this time, the text has stayed the same, but views of it have changed, along with changing fashions in writing. Below are some of the praise and criticisms that *Treasure Island* has attracted over the years.

1881 (When it was serialized as *The Sea Cook*)
"It's not like other books for boys"

1883 (When it was first published as a book)
"Great imagination!"
"Great characters!"

1894 (Following the death of Stevenson)
"Our Prince of Storytellers has gone"

1914–1950
"His work is childish"
"Quaint"
"Old-fashioned"
"Hollow"

1950–2000
"Exciting – like flying"
"Sheer pleasure"
"Thrilling!"

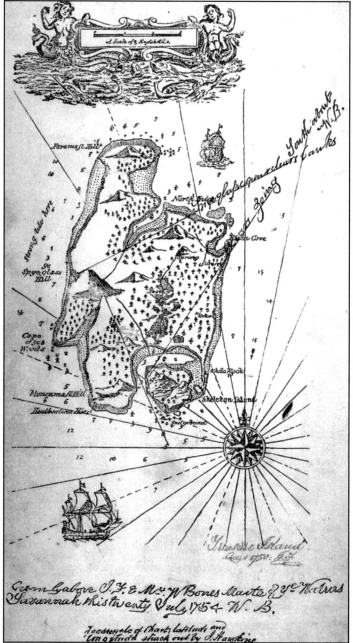

The original map of Treasure Island, as drawn by Stevenson.

TIMELINE OF WORLD EVENTS

DURING THE LIFETIME OF ROBERT LOUIS STEVENSON

1850
November 13th - Robert Louis Balfour Stevenson is born.
Thousands rush to California after gold is discovered.

1851
Herman Melville writes his whaling adventure, *Moby Dick*.

1853
Crimean War starts.

1858
India becomes part of British Empire.
First telegraph (signals) cable under Atlantic Ocean.

1859
Work begins on digging Suez Canal (Egypt) to link Mediterranean Sea to Red Sea and Indian Ocean.
Small states unite to create nation of Italy.
Charles Darwin writes his first book on evolution, *On the Origin of Species*.

1861
American Civil War begins, between states for and against slavery.
Louis Pasteur discovers bacteria.

1865
American Civil War ends and slavery banned.
President Abraham Lincoln assassinated.
Jospeh Lister uses antiseptic to reduce infections after surgery.
Gregor Mendel makes pioneering study of genetics.

1866
Alfred Nobel invents dynamite.
America purchases Alaska from Russia.

1867
Stevenson attends Edinburgh University to study engineering.

1868
Revolution in Spain.

1871
Stevenson changes studies from engineering to law.

1875
Stevenson qualifies as a lawyer.

1876
Alexander Graham Bell invents telephone.

1878
Stevenson's first volume of work is published, *An Inland Voyage* – a piece of travel writing.

1879
Thomas Edison invents electric light.

1880
Stevenson marries Fanny Van De Grift Osbourne.

1881
Stevenson and Fanny go to Scotland.
The Sea Cook is published in *Young Folks*.

1883
Treasure Island is published as a book.

1886
Arthur Conan Doyle writes first story about detective hero Sherlock Holmes.
The Strange Case of Dr. Jekyll and Mr. Hyde is published.
Kidnapped is published.

1887
George Eastman invents box camera.
Stevenson and Fanny return to America.

1889
Eiffel Tower is built.
Stevenson and his family arrive and settle on Samoa, an island in the Pacific Ocean.
The Master of Ballantrae is published.

1894
December 3rd – Robert Louis Stevenson dies in Samoa at age 44.

Robert Louis Stevenson also wrote a huge amount of poetry, essays, and travel writing as well as the novels for which he is best known.

STAGE, SCREEN - AND PUPPETS

FILMS AND TELEVISION

Jhe printed text of *Treasure Island* has also been transformed into an astonishing number of films, TV series, radio broadcasts, and stage plays. These have been adapted and performed worldwide, in languages ranging from Russian to Japanese.

The first stage script was prepared in 1902 and the first film in 1908. A Hollywood version, made in 1934 with an all-star cast, was very popular – although some critics dismissed it as "hokum." It was remade and became the first live-action film made by Disney studios in 1950, attracting even larger audiences. Since then, there have been several other major Hollywood-TV coproductions. Probably the best television film (1989) starred Charlton Heston as Long John Silver, with Blind Pew memorably played by veteran horror-film actor Christopher Lee.

There have also been cartoon versions (in films and books), computer games – and a *Treasure Island* musical. In one

in Japan in 1971) the characters were replaced by animals. In another (*Muppet Treasure Island*, 1996) the story was acted by kooky puppets. Some directors have faithfully followed Robert Louis Stevenson's original story, but others have changed it dramatically. For example, in both the 1987 TV series starring Anthony Quinn and *Treasure Planet* (Disney, 2002), the story is set in space.

Captain Blood *starring Errol Flynn, 1935*

Individual character traits from *Treasure Island* have also featured in many films, books, and plays. Not long after Stevenson's death, playwrite James Barrie created *Peter Pan* (1904) for children. It starred a character called Captain Hook, a vicious pirate with a parrot. *Captain Blood* (1935) starred Errol Flynn as a charismatic buccaneer and is still considered one of the best pirate

films ever made. British journalist Arthur Ransome wrote novels (such as *Swallows and Amazons*, 1930) about brothers and sisters who played at pirates and then had real-life adventures. Books for older readers, like William Golding's sinister *Lord of the Flies* (1959), explore ideas – like being marooned – borrowed from *Treasure Island*. More recently, international film stars like Johnny Depp have achieved great success in entertaining, light-hearted films such as *Pirates of the Caribbean* (2003). These usually feature cruel but likeable heroes, inspired by Long John Silver.

Johnny Depp as Captain Jack Sparrow in Pirates of the Caribbean, *2003*

OTHER NOVELS BY ROBERT LOUIS STEVENSON

1878 – *An Inland Voyage*
1879 – *Travels with a Donkey in the Cévennes*
1883 – *Treasure Island*
1884 – *The Silverado Squatters*
1885 – *A Child's Garden of Verses*
1885 – *The Body Snatcher*
1886 – *Kidnapped*

1886 – *The Strange Case of Dr. Jekyll and Mr. Hyde*
1888 – *The Black Arrow*
1889 – *The Master of Ballantrae*
1892 – *The Wrong Box*
1896 – *Weir of Hermiston* (published posthumously; Stevenson was working on this the day he died)

INDEX

IF YOU LIKED THIS BOOK, YOU MIGHT ALSO WANT TO TRY THESE TITLES IN THE BARRON'S *GRAPHIC CLASSICS* SERIES:

The Hunchback of Notre Dame
Journey to the Center of the Earth
Kidnapped
Moby Dick
Oliver Twist

FOR MORE INFORMATION ON ROBERT LOUIS STEVENSON:

The National Library of Scotland
www.nls.uk

Stevenson House
www.stevenson-house.co.uk